Get Fit with VIDEO Workouts

DANCE & FITNESS
TRENDS

Sue
Davis
Potts

Mitchell Lane
PUBLISHERS
P.O. Box 196
Hockessin, DE 19707

African Dance Trends
Get Fit with Video Workouts
Line Dances Around the World
Trends in Hip-Hop Dance
Trends in Martial Arts
The World of CrossFit
Yoga Fitness
Zumba Fitness

Printing
1 2 3 4 5 6 7 8 9

Library of Congress
Cataloging-in-Publication Data

Sue Davis Potts
  Get fit with video workouts / by Sue Davis Potts.
        pages cm. — (Dance and fitness trends)
  Includes bibliographical references and index.
  Includes webography.
  Audience: Age: 9-13.
  Audience: Grade: 4 to 8.
  ISBN 978-1-61228-550-4 (library bound)
  1. Physical fitness—Juvenile literature.
  2. Video recordings—Juvenile literature. I. Title.
  GV481.P597 2014
  613.7—dc23
                                                      2014008300

eBook ISBN: 9781612285900

Contents

The fitness industry is a fast-growing and fast-changing industry that is expected to see continued growth. What initially many thought was just a fad quickly spread like wildfire. Even the fitness pioneers themselves were surprised at the success that they had in this market. With the promise of the latest and greatest products, trainers and instructors rode the fitness train to wealth.

The introduction of the exercise video pushed fitness to a whole new level and made it more accessible to everyone—even people who had never worked out before. In turn, this interest in personal health boosted the drive to develop more workout gyms, equipment, and personal trainers, creating

Introduction

more and more careers in the fitness world. To keep up with the times, the world of fitness has had to make its way into technology with games and apps. The exercise video that initially was marketed to stay-at-home mothers has evolved to include people of all ages and fitness levels. Ways to stay healthy are more and more available—as are the choices to make it fun.

With so much out there, how do you choose the program or product that is right for you and your fitness needs? What are the latest trends? How has the fitness industry adapted to the changing times and the technology age?

Actress Jane Fonda became well-known for her workout videos in the 1980s.

Chapter 1
Not Just a Fad

Dresses with shoulder pads, big hair with the Farrah Fawcett flip, and chain belts were some of the fashion and beauty fads of the 1980s. People were also becoming obsessed with getting physically fit. Actress and political activist Jane Fonda had danced ballet all of her life to stay in shape until a foot injury in her forties prevented her from dancing, and she began gaining weight. She called a friend to help her find another workout method. The program worked for her, and in 1981 she wrote a book about her fitness routine called *Jane Fonda's Workout Book*. According to Fonda, Debbie Karl, the wife of video pioneer Stuart Karl, read her book and told her husband that he should ask Fonda to do an exercise video. Up until that time Karl had mostly produced home-improvement videos. The VCR had been invented years earlier but was just getting affordable enough so that ordinary people could own one in their home. Karl took his wife's advice and asked Fonda to do an aerobic workout video. Aerobic means "using oxygen." When done on a regular basis and with enough energy, this type of exercise keeps the heart and lungs in good condition. It works all areas of fitness flexibility, muscle strength, and the cardiovascular system. Fonda said no to Karl at first because she thought making a fitness video would be bad for her career, but she finally agreed to do it for the proceeds to go to a political organization she had founded.

That trailblazing video, *Workout: Starring Jane Fonda*, was released in 1982. Not only did sales of Fonda's video skyrocket, it also boosted the sales of VCRs. People were buying the machines just so they could play Fonda's video and exercise

Jack LaLanne, known as the "Godfather of Fitness," in a 1986 photo at the age of 71.

along with her at home. Fonda was soon as well known for her workout video as for her acting and added fitness guru to her title of accomplishments. As of 2012, the thirtieth anniversary of the first video, it had sold 17 million copies.

While Fonda may have created the first workout video, exercise shows had been on TV some thirty years before. The Jack LaLanne show began in 1951 and featured fitness, health, and nutrition expert Jack LaLanne. The show reached out to stay-at-home housewives and mothers, motivating women to exercise and take time to improve their fitness. It aired for thirty-four years, earning LaLanne the nickname "Godfather of Fitness." Along with exercise LaLanne offered advice on how to be healthier and feel better. He is also credited with opening one of the first fitness gyms in the United States in 1936. LaLanne died at the age of 96 in 2011, said to still be exercising until the day before he died.

Richard Simmons soon danced through the VHS-workout door that Jane Fonda had opened, with his *Sweatin' to the Oldies* video in 1988. Simmons, who had been an overweight teen, had lost the weight and kept it off and was now on a mission to help others lose weight, get healthy, and have a fun time doing it. He combined popular songs with his exercise routines, which made exercise entertaining and less like work. Simmons's unforgettable style—a combination of afro, striped shorty shorts, and bright colors often accented with glitter—made him an icon of the '80s. His energetic, fun routines coupled with his ability to make people feel like he cared about them individually propelled his success. He burst on the video and television scene with such energy that he soon became a household name.

Other workouts such as Jazzersize—an energetic workout set to jazz music, created by professional dancer Judi Sheppard Missett in 1969—found a place in the video market as well. Step aerobics helped round out the fitness routines of the '80s. This workout added another element to regular aerobics by adding a riser or step used to step on and off of during exercise.

Much of the early fitness world was focused on women. The American Heart Association states that cardiovascular disease or heart disease is the greatest health risk for women. They recommend a heart-healthy lifestyle to decrease the likelihood of getting heart disease. That lifestyle would include making healthy eating choices and exercising regularly, which includes finding a workout that's right for you. The fitness

A group of women participate in a Jazzercize class. Jazzercize combines dance, strength training, yoga, Pilates, and kickboxing for a total body workout.

industry may not have been of aware of these warnings when it first started, but workout videos improved their health focus as time went on.

Whatever motivation was behind it, fitness became a new adventure for many—and the start of a craze that made for big business and new careers never before possible. It was soon something that everyone wanted in on: creating a world where you could make a lifestyle and a living out of fitness.

The Advantages and Disadvantages of Using Workout Videos

Unlike today, when workout videos first came out, you couldn't find gyms or exercise classes in every town. One of the benefits that drove the popularity of this means of exercise was convenience: you could exercise right in your living room. But now that Planet Fitness gyms and Zumba classes, for example, are seemingly everywhere, what are the advantages and disadvantages of video workouts?

Advantages
- Convenience: You can work out any time of the day or night.
- Privacy: Some people are embarrassed to work out with others.
- Variety: You can change workouts and types of exercise so that you don't burn out or get bored with one particular kind of exercise.
- Less expensive: A few videos cost less than a membership to a gym and the gas to get there.

Disadvantages
- No support group: A group exercise class offers you the support of others in the class with you. Participants of class workouts can encourage each other when they are tempted to give up.
- No accountability: If you don't show up for a class, you will be missed. Usually no one will know if you skip your video workout.
- No feedback from the Instructor: A class instructor can give a participant immediate correction if an exercise is being done incorrectly.
- It requires self-discipline: Some people are unable to motivate themselves to do video exercising on a regular basis. It's easy to get distracted at home by chores that need to get done, and we never seem to find the time to work out.
- Choosing the wrong workout for you: Trainers and instructors know how to choose workouts based on needs and ability levels.

Singer-choreographer Paula Abdul released many dance work-out videos throughout her career.

Chapter 2
The Fitness Explosion

The 1990s saw a surge of exercise videos and TV shows, each promising that their method was the best at achieving the goal of weight loss and muscle tone. Many guaranteed easier workouts and faster results for a healthier, better-looking body. For some fitness pros it was a true desire to help others, for some it was a way to boost their career in the health market, but for others it was just a way to make money.

Just as video sales surged, so did the building of fitness gyms for those who wanted a personal trainer and didn't want to go it alone. Many of these personal trainers started combining bits and pieces of different programs to fit the needs of their clients. This led many trainers to release videos of their own.

The first health-focused TV channel began in 1993, when televangelist Pat Robertson started Cable Health Club, which then became known as Fitness TV. In 2011 it merged with America's Health Network to become Discovery Fit and Health.

Numerous celebrities also began jumping on the fitness bandwagon to offer their videos and products—singer and actress Cher, model Cindy Crawford, singer-dancer Paula Abdul, then-teen actress Alyssa Milano, and body builder Tony Little to name a few.

Little had been unable to continue doing his usual body-building routine due to a car accident, leading him to invent the Gazelle. The Gazelle is a low-impact aerobic machine that accompanied Little's *Total Body Workout* video, and he soon became well-known for his infomercials to sell this machine.

Tony Little demonstrates his Easy Shaper
Total Body Exerciser resistance bands.

Yoga (with a capital *Y*) is a spiritual way of life associated with Eastern religions. Originating in India, it has been around for centuries. Yoga teaches how to suppress all activity of the body and the mind. By contrast, yoga (with a lower-case *y*) first gained popularity in the 1990s and uses a series of poses with breathing exercises and meditation to relax the body and teach focus. The practice of yoga focuses on the complete person: mind, body, and spirit. Yoga movements range from shifting eye exercises to standing on your head. It is designed to encourage a healthy lifestyle and a peaceful mind.

One of the most popular, longest-lasting fitness programs is Tae-Bo, created by Billy Blanks in the 1990s. Blanks describes The Tae-Bo Way as a total workout of the mind, body, and spirit—much like yoga although far more active. Tae-Bo is a combination of martial arts, dance, and boxing. Blanks states that "tae" is the Korean word for *foot* or to strike with the foot (as in "tae kwan do"), and "bo" is the short form of the word *box*. He says that he chose this name because many of the movements of this program focus on the lower body. Blanks also developed an anagram to describe what Tae-Bo stands for to him.

T represents total commitment to whatever you do.
A represents awareness of yourself and the world.
E represents excellence, the truest goal in anything you do.
B represents the body as a force for total change.
O represents obedience to your will and your true desire to change.

Growing up the fourth child of fifteen, Blanks had sizable obstacles in his way to success such as poverty, shyness, a problem with a hip tendon, and undiagnosed dyslexia. He gives much credit for his success to his parents, his faith, and finding karate when he was twelve. He has been recognized as a seven-time karate world champion and

Billy Blanks, creator of Tae Bo, instructed a class in 2006 at the Fleet Recreation Center for active-duty personnel stationed at Commander, Fleet Activities Yokosuka, Japan.

captain of the 1980 United States Karate Team. In 1989 he began as a personal trainer in The Billy Blanks World Karate Center, and there he developed Tae-Bo.

Fitness Careers

According to the *Occupational Outlook Handbook*, jobs for fitness trainers and instructors are on the rise. Places of employment for trainers and instructors include health clubs, country clubs, fitness or recreation centers, gyms, hospitals, universities, yoga and Pilate's studios, resorts, and clients' homes.

Most of these jobs have an entry-level education requirement of a high school diploma or the equivalent, and short-term on-the-job training is usually essential. Training differs depending on the specific area of fitness that the job involves. The probability of getting a job in this field increases with higher levels of education and certifications in health and fitness.

According to the U.S. Department of Labor Bureau of Labor Statistics, as of 2012, the average pay for this type of career was $31,720 per year or $15.25 per hour. Employment for these occupations is expected to increase 13 percent in the time period 2012 to 2022, which is average growth across the board in the American job market. As more employers and insurance companies encourage their employees and clients to join fitness programs, and as more people take advantage of these programs, the need for instructors and trainers will rise.

Other physical-fitness careers are coaches, physical-education teachers, athletic trainers, physical therapists, and recreational workers. These jobs usually require at least a college degree or some college plus on-the-job training. Like careers for trainers or fitness instructors, these jobs are also expected to see an increase in job availability over the next few years.

Josh Reynolds demonstrates an upper-body exercise using his 1992 invention the ThighMaster. This popular piece of exercise equipment, touted by Suzanne Somers in infomercials, had over $100 million in sales.

Chapter 3
Big Business

Actress Suzanne Somers, best known for playing a not-so-smart character on the TV show *Three's Company*, was very smart when it came to the business world of exercise. She was one of the first celebrities to promote a fitness product when she endorsed the ThighMaster. This device was placed between the knees and squeezed for resistance training to develop and tone thigh muscles—although critics of the ThighMaster felt that it was more a gimmick than an actual piece of fitness equipment. The ThighMaster was billed to be a spot-reduction aid. In other words, if you used it, fat would come off your thighs. Fitness experts argued that while you may tone muscle in a certain area, exercise does not remove fat from one particular area. The ThighMaster sold in record numbers and so did several updated versions. This gadget is still being sold today under various names.

Somers primarily promoted the ThighMaster though TV infomercials. These infomercials usually ranged from a few minutes in length up to a half hour. The endorser demonstrates how the product works and tries to convince viewers that their life will be better and that they cannot live without the item. Infomercials are a direct way of advertising that allows the customer to pick up the phone and order a product immediately. Suzanne Somers's ThighMaster and Tony Little's Gazelle were just a couple of the early exercise items sold in addition to workout videos. Although fitness-related products were by far not the only things sold by infomercial, it was one of the fastest-growing areas in this form of advertising and included

Infomercials continue to bring in sales for exercise equipment and products, such as the Power Rider, demonstrated here.

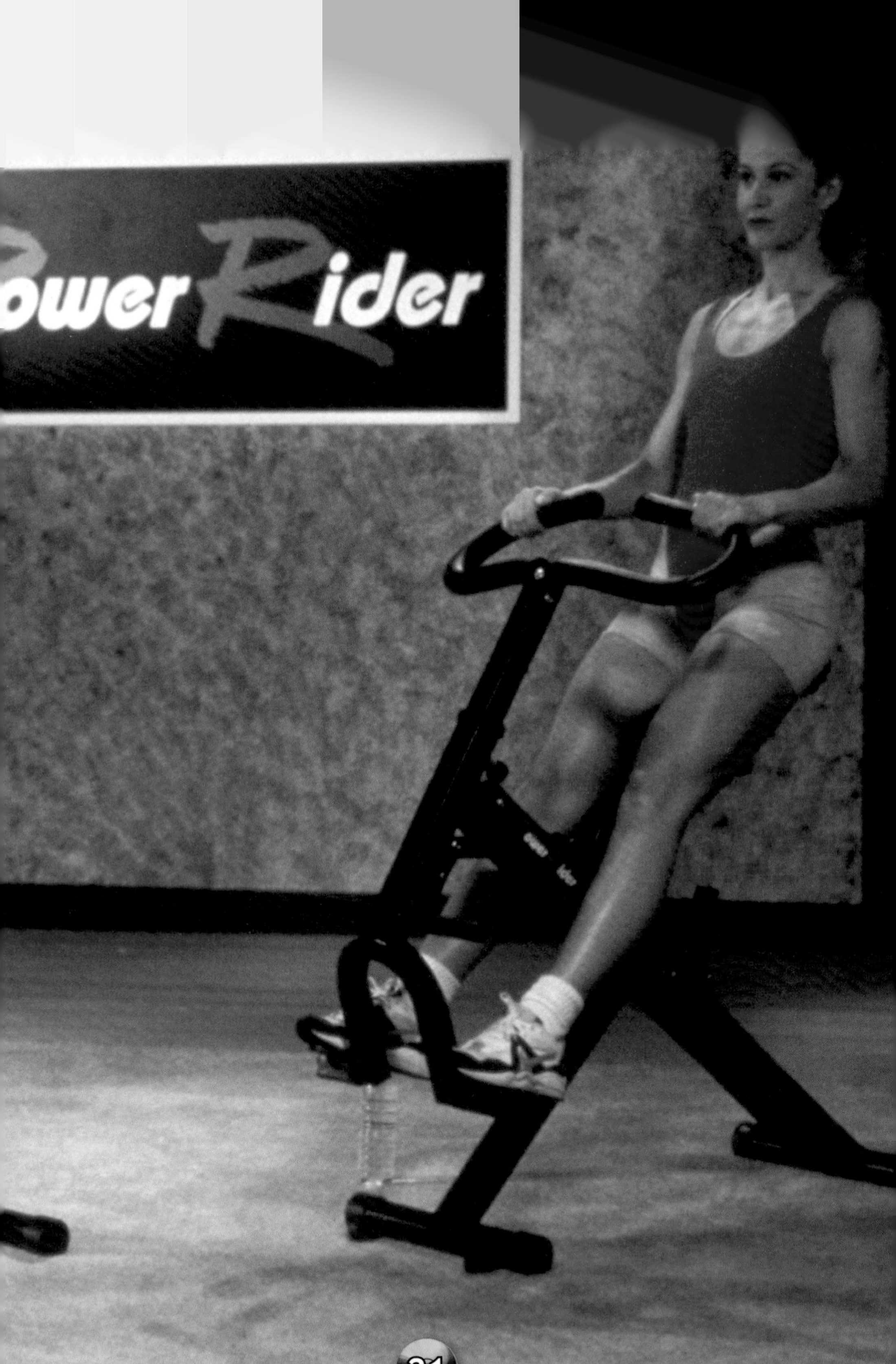
owerRider

other popular fitness trends like the Abdomenizer and the *Buns of Steel* workout videos.

Throughout the '90s not only were videos selling in the millions but also the products that went along with them. Some of this merchandise was for fashion: to look good while

Healthy eating is a necessary part of staying fit.

exercising to look better. Things such as leg warmers, leotards, and sweatbands made the statement that you were serious about working out. And shoes were endorsed by major sports stars as must-haves for exercise—even if it was just walking. Some things were simple like weights, yoga mats, and an

exercise ball that you sat on to bounce yourself fit. Others were more complex. Home-gym and weights-equipment endorsers claimed that if you purchased their apparatus, you could have gym-membership results in the convenience of your own home.

Most exercise gurus agree that eating right is an important part of staying fit, so diets and food programs were sold along with the videos. Richard Simmons not only profited from his nine books and sixty-five fitness videos, but he also developed the Deal-A-Meal and FoodMover weight-loss programs that help participants count calories and measure portion sizes. Deal-A-Meal was a set of cards dictating the food groups and you should eat, in a day. The goal start out with cards on one side plastic holder that came with the and as you eat you transfer that card to the other side of the holder. When the cards allotted for the day were all transferred to other side, you were through day.

Gyms and health clubs were opening up everywhere, giving an increased opportunity for jobs in the fitness industry. Many who could afford it were seeking personal trainers to help them on their fitness journey, and it seemed as if everyone was getting certi-fied and becoming an expert in something.

Making an Exercise Video

Are you interested in making your own workout video? If so, consider putting your creation on YouTube. Putting a video on YouTube will get your name and face before the public. Popular videos sometimes have millions of viewers! And who knows? If you become a hit on YouTube, this might even get the attention of a video producer who could help you create a professional video to sell.

Begin by making a plan. Choose a location. Will it be outside, in a gym, or a room in your house? Decide what exercises and how many you want to include in your video. It would probably be a good idea to write a script for your introduction and instructions to make sure you don't leave out anything important. If you want it to be a dance video, choose your music. Make it even more fun by asking your friends to join in and exercise along with you.

Now that you are all set, give it a few practice runs. It might help to practice in front of a mirror. When you think you are ready, record your production, and get it posted online. Enjoy seeing something that you created! And your video will not only help you and your friends but also other kids who will watch it to stay healthy and keep fit.

A woman exercises at home using a workout video.

Chapter 4

How Do You Choose the Right Workout Video?

With so many choices, how do you choose a video that is right for you? When choosing a video, several areas need to be considered, such as intensity level, type of workout, time required, equipment and cost, preference, and suitability.

When thinking about intensity level, physical fitness and activity ability need to be a concern. For a person who has never exercised before, it would be dangerous to start with a high-intensity workout. Choosing a type of workout involves deciding if you want a full-body workout or an exercise that concentrates on one particular area such as the abs.

Preference is a big part of choosing a workout program. After all, if you don't like it, you are not likely to do it. This is why dance videos flood the market. You may choose to do fitness program that doesn't involve music, but if you do choose a dance video, you can select one for the type of music that you enjoy. Along with Jazzersize, which focuses on jazz music, and Richard Simmons's *Sweatin' to the Oldies*, there are videos featuring almost any kind of music imaginable, from classical to hip hop to reggae. If you want to add a spiritual dimension, you can work out to Christian praise music or gospel music. Country music fans can choose a line-dance video. Or try the newer Latin craze of Zumba.

Even ballroom dancing has a place in the fitness world, thanks to the popular TV show *Dancing with the Stars*. Many of the celebrity contestants on the show boast of weight loss while training and participating in the show. Not surprisingly, the *Dancing with the Stars Cardio Fit* was released in 2006 by the show, and several of the show's pro dancers—like Julianne

Hough, Cheryl Burke, and Kym Johnson—have put out their
own videos.

Another factor to consider when choosing a workout video
is the time and money that you have to put into it. What
equipment is needed to do the program correctly? Can you fit
in a full hour or ninety-minute workout, or do you need a
shorter plan?

Kym Johnson, Maksim Chmerkovskiy, and Ashly DelGrosso are three of the professional dancers on TV's popular *Dancing with the Stars* who have helped in the making of the show's workout videos.

There are also videos for different age groups and for those with special needs and the physically challenged. Many fitness trainers who had success in the general market went back and made more specialized videos, such as Tony Horton's video *Tony and the Kids* and Denise Austin's *Fit Kids*. As always, the most important thing to consider before any exercise program is your health.

TV Fitness trainer Jillian Michaels launched her *Fitness Ultimatum* computer game in 2010.

Some other choices for kid's videos are *Yoga Kids: Vol. 2 ABC's for Ages 3-6*, *Get Fit and Fab with Jillian Michaels*, *Shaun T's Fit Kids Club DVD Workout*, and *Billy Blanks Tae-Bo Kicks*. If you prefer a dance workout, you might try *Hip Hop for Kids: School House Hip Hop* or *Dance X: Fun Dance & Exercise for Kids with Great Music*. These are just a few of the possibilities. Before you choose, go online and type in "Kids exercise DVDS" in the search box, and spend some time picking out the one that is just right for you.

Exercise Tips

Have you have decided to begin an exercise program? Congratulations on making a great choice about your health. Before you begin, here are a few tips to help you stay safe while you work on staying fit.

- Eat healthy! Starvation diets and not getting proper nutrition can lead to major health problems.
- Drink plenty of water. Dehydration leads to exhaustion and muscle cramps.
- Warm up before an exercise routine, and cool down after exercising.
- Choose a program that is right for your fitness and activity level, and start slowly. Trying to do too much at first will lead to burnout.
- Don't overwork your muscles. Overdoing it can lead to injuries. Pace yourself, and stop if you are in pain. Changing up the type of exercise can also help prevent overworking one group of muscles.
- Make sure that you use equipment and products correctly, and have proper supervision.
- For best results, use an exercise program the way that it was designed to be used by the expert who designed it.
- Exercise with the right attitude. Do it because you want to get healthier and feel better. Don't do it only to look good or because of someone else's opinion. Be proud of yourself, and acknowledge when you have reached your exercise goals.
- If you feel severe chest pain, or if you have an actual injury, find an adult to ask for help, or stop and call 911.

Check with your doctor before beginning an exercise program. This is especially important if you have a health condition that might limit certain activities or if the program you are beginning is strenuous compared to your current daily activity level.

First Lady Michelle Obama began the *Let's Move* campaign to fight childhood obesity and promote a healthy lifestyle. She gets involved in the program herself as is seen here in 2013 in New York.

Chapter 5
The Latest Trends

On February 9, 2010, First Lady Michelle Obama began the *Let's Move* campaign. Statistics show that one in three children in the United States is obese or overweight. Mrs. Obama attributes this to fewer activities, not only because school physical education programs are being cut but also because children are spending more at home time inside instead of outside playing. Plus less food is homegrown and home cooked, and portion sizes have increased along with snacking. *Let's Move* recommends that kids get one hour of moderate to vigorous physical activity every day, which can include dance and fitness programs.

Let's Move statistics include the estimate that in a typical day, kids eight to eighteen spend an average of 7.5 hours on entertainment media, including TV, videos, computers, cell phones, and movies. The exercise industry has taken advantage of the time that kids spend on media with fitness simulator games. These usually fall into five categories: Dance-Based Games, Simulation Sports, Virtual Cycling, Martial Arts Games, and Gamercize.

The dance-based games allow participants to follow along with the dance moves on the screen. In the *Dance Dance Revolution* game, players stand on a dance pad that allows their movements to be graded. In 2009 Wii also released *Just Dance*, a dance-along where using the Wii remote allows points to be recorded.

The simulated-sports area of gaming devices is also a popular trend of the last few years. The Wii Fit uses gaming controls to play virtual sports such as tennis, bowling, or

At E3 2012, the Electronic Entertainment Expo held on June 8, 2012, in Los Angeles, California, professional dancers demonstrate Dance Central 3 for Kinect and Xbox 360.

35

boxing. When the movements of swinging at a ball or other sports-related motions are made, the device lets the player know if the action was within the standards of the game. Along with the handheld device, a balance board is added for simulation of more advanced sports such as skateboarding or snowboarding.

Kids in Ukraine participate in an athletics competition in 2012. The program encourages healthy activities for kids.

Virtual cycling use exercise bikes connected to monitors that allows players to use handlebars and peddles to control or respond to what is happening onscreen. Leg muscles are strengthened when cycling is done on a regular basis, and it can be a good cardiovascular workout. Virtual cycling devices include Cateye Fitness and GameBike.

Technology is one of the many aids available today to help with workout programs.

Martial arts games teach endurance and strength and improve coordination and reaction time. Xbox released the best-known martial arts games with the 2010 release of Kinect. This game freed the player from having to hold a remote by detecting movements through motion sensors.

The weight-loss TV show *The Biggest Loser* has shone a light on one of the biggest names in fitness training in this decade. Jillian Michaels has released over fifteen videos since the show first aired in 2004. Her latest video, released in 2012, is titled *Jillian Michaels Body Revolution*, promising to transform your body in ninety days.

One of the most popular fitness programs trending now is Zumba. This fitness program was developed in the 1990s by Alberto "Beto" Perez in Colombia with dances choreographed to Latin music. In 2001 Perez moved to the United States and began teaching Zumba®, and ever since, Zumba has been gaining in popularity. According to the Zumba website, fourteen million participants in 185 countries are doing Zumba. In 2012 Zumba Fitness was named *Inc.* magazine's Company of the Year.

Two other hot trends of recent years are *P90X* and *Insanity*, both products of the Beachbody Fitness Company. *P90X* was created by Tony Horton and released in 2004. *Insanity* was created by Shaun T and released in 2009. Another version titled *Insanity: The Asylum* was released in 2011. These programs are billed as being for the extremely fit. They are high-impact, strenuous exercises designed to get drastic results in a short period of time.

Speaking of extremes, a much simpler and less-intense form of exercise has risen in popularity. Hooping has seen new growth recently largely due to Christabel Zamor, creator of *HoopGirl Workout*. She has taken the 1950s hula-hoop fad to a new level and credits the hoop with helping her to lose weight, de-stress, and even stop smoking. Zamor believes hooping results in improvements in core strength, motor skills,

Hooping

and flexibility. She also stresses, as do many other instructors, the mind-and-spirit benefits such as laughter, creativity, and self-esteem.

The fitness industry was not to be left behind when the technology-age dawned. Not only were the type of exercises, such as gaming, changing, but so was the way they were distributed. Online work-out programs were developed. Programs such as iBodyfit.com and MyYoga-Online.com were easily accessible. Now instead of popping in a video or DVD, you could sign up to have your workout pop up on your computer screen. Even more recently, workouts can be accessed with an app for your mobile phone. With apps such *iPump Fitness Builder, You Are Your Own Gym,* and *iMapMyFit-ness,* your workout can go everywhere you go.

With all the changes and modern updates, many fitness gurus can easily make a lifelong commitment to staying fit and helping others do so as well. When Jane Fonda released her first video in 1982, she had no idea of the impact that she would have. It's probably safe to say that she also had no idea that some thirty years later, at the age of seventy-five, she would still be releasing workout DVDs now geared to the health needs of senior citizens and baby boomers.

Children Staying Fit

As Michelle Obama points out in the *Let's Move* campaign, childhood obesity is a nationwide problem and if not dealt with will lead to lifelong health problems such as heart disease and diabetes. According to the Centers for Disease Control and Prevention, childhood obesity has more than doubled in children and tripled in adolescents in the past thirty years.

While the solution to this problem will be a joint effort by parents, schools, communities, and health and fitness experts, there are some steps that kids can follow to stay healthy:

- Eat a balanced diet. Lower your intake of sugary, starchy junk foods.
- Exercise. While video and gaming exercises are a good place to start, add other exercises like walking, running, bike riding, and playing sports.
- Do not go on fad diets or starve yourself hoping to lose weight. These diets seldom work, and if they do, you will probably gain back the weight as fast as you lost it.
- Assist in fixing healthy snacks and meals for yourself.
- Ask for help. Talk to your parents about your concerns. Talk to teachers and school officials about programs to see if there are programs that could be implemented to help you reach your fitness goals. Consult your family doctor or a nutritionist if needed.
- Believe in yourself. No matter what fitness or weight level you are, you can make positive changes toward a healthier you.

If you would like to start a video workout, begin by deciding what style of exercise you would like to do. Do you want to dance? Do you prefer a gaming workout? Ask yourself if you have the discipline to do a workout by yourself or if you need the support of a group or trainer.

Some things to consider are cost, equipment needed, and time. After you have an idea of the type of program you would like, look on the Internet to see what's available. The Internet is also a good source to find the price of home videos and equipment, and it will give you endless options and information to help you choose the program that is right for you. You can also call local gyms in your area to see if they offer the type of program that you are interested in.

If you are looking for a class and can't find any kid's programs in your area, ask the adult instructors if they or someone they know could start a kid's class. You could also check with your school and see if they would consider starting a program at school.

Choose a program that will help you stay fit and healthy—but also choose one that is fun. If you consider something to be fun, even though it will be challenging, you will be more likely to stick with it. Be sure that your parents approve of your choice and if you have any medical issues that your doctor has given the go-ahead for your workout.

1951	*The Jack LaLanne Show* begins.
1982	Jane Fonda releases her first video, *Workout: Starring Jane Fonda*.
1988	Richard Simmons releases his first video, *Sweatin' to the Oldies*.
1990	TV infomercials begin selling fitness programs and products.
1993	Cable Health Club begins.
1999	Billy Blanks's Tae-Bo is released.
2001	Alberto Perez begins the Zumba fitness program in the United States.
2004	P90X is released.
2006	*Dancing with the Stars Cardio Fit* video is released.
2007	Wii Fit is released.
2009	iPump 20 sends the first workout clips to cell phones.
2010	First Lady Michelle Obama inaugurates the *Let's Move* campaign. Jane Fonda releases the first of her *Prime Time* videos.
2011	Fitness pioneer Jack LaLanne dies at the age of 96.
2012	Jane Fonda celebrates the thirtieth anniversary of the release of her first workout video.
2012	Apple releases the *Zombies, Run!* app, and it becomes the number-one top grossing health and fitness app on Apple's App Store.
2013	Microsoft releases *Bing Heath & Fitness*—an app that tracks diet, health, and exercise—for all Windows devices.
2014	Casio releases a new sports watch that's compatible with mobile fitness apps.

Books

Blanks, Billy. *The Tae-Bo Way*. New York: Bantam Books, 1999.

Zamor, Christabel. *Hooping: A Revolutionary Fitness Program*. New York: Workman Publishing. 2009.

On the Internet

Alsac, Biray. *IDEA Health & Fitness Association,* "Game On," February 2009. http://www.ideafit.com/fitness-library/game-on

Arney, Juliane. *IDEA Health & Fitness Association,* "You Should Be in Pictures," January 2005. http://www.ideafit.com/fitness-library/you-should-be-pictures-0

Crosby, Olivia. *Occupational Outlook Quarterly,* "Working So Others Can Play: Jobs in Video Game Development," Summer 2000, vol. 44, no. 2. http://www.bls.gov/opub/ooq/2000/summer/art01.htm

Works Consulted

American Heart Association, *Complete Guide to Women's Heart Health*. New York: Clarkson/Potter Publishers, 2009.

Blanks, Billy. *The Tae-Bo Way*. New York: Bantam Books, 1999.

Fonda, Jane. *Jane Fonda,* "30th Anniversary of My First Workout Video," April 24, 2012. http://janefonda.com/30th-anniversary-of-my-first-workout-video

"Jack LaLanne," *Biography.com,* April 24, 2014. http://www.biography.com/people/jack-lalanne-273648

Kids.gov, "Exercise, Fitness, and Nutrition." http://kids.usa.gov/grown-ups/exercise-fitness-nutrition/index.shtml

LaLanne, Jack. *Jack LaLanne,* "About Jack." http://www.jacklalanne.com/jacks-adventures/

Let's Move, "America's Move to Raise a Healthier Generation of Kids." http://www.letsmove.gov

Liming, Drew and Vilorio, Dennis. *Occupational Outlook Quarterly,* "Work for Play: Careers in Video Game Development," Fall 2011, vol. 55, no. 3. http://www.bls.gov/opub/ooq/2011/fall/

Miller, Ivan. *Outside,* "Workout Videos: Stretching the Limit of Fitness Programming," May 4, 2009. http://www.outsideonline.com/outdoor-adventure/media/film/Workout-Videos.html

Narcisse, Evan. *Time,* "+1 to Health: American Heart Association Gives Nintendo Stamp of Approval," May 17, 2010. http://techland.time.com/2010/05/17/1-to-health-american-heart-association-gives-nintendo-stamp-of-approval/

Park, Alice. *Time,* "Want Your Kids to Exercise? Let Them Play Video Games!" March 7, 2011. http://healthland.time.com/2011/03/07/want-your-kids-to-exercise-let-them-play-video-games/

President's Challenge, "Presidential Youth Fitness Program." https://www.presidentschallenge.org/

Richard Simmons.com, "A Biography of Richard Simmons," http://www.richardsimmons.com/site/richards-bio

Sivananda Yoga Vendanta Center, *Yoga Mind and Body.* New York: DK Publishing, 2008.

Zamor, Christabel. *Hooping: A Revolutionary Fitness Program.* New York: Workman Publishing, 2009.

PHOTO CREDITS: All design elements from Thinkstock/Sharon Beck; Cover, pp. 1, 24,40—Photos.com/Thinkstock; pp. 4-5, 38—Syda Productions/Dreamstime; p. 6—Denis Makarenko/Dreamstime; p. 8—WireImage/Getty Images; pp. 10, 12, 32—Dreamstime; p. 14—AR4 WENN Photos/Newscom; p. 16—Photographer's Mate 1st Class Crystal Brooks/US Navy; pp. 17, 25, 26, 41—Thinkstock; p. 18—Jebb Harris/ZUMA Press/Newscom; pp. 20-21—Time & Life Pictures/Getty Images; pp. 22-23—Gpointstudio/Dreamstime; pp. 28-29—Getty Images; p. 30—Anton Oparin/Dreamstime; pp. 34-35—Antonio Jodice/Dreamstime; pp. 36-37—Denys Kuvaiev/Dreamstime; p. 42—Vladimir Grigorev/Dreamstime.

aerobic (er-OH-bik)—In exercise, increasing oxygen use by making the body work harder.

bandwagon (BAND-wag-uhn)—A popular activity or movement that attracts many followers.

cardiovascular (CAR-dee-oh-VAS-kyuh-ler)—Pertaining to or affecting the heart and blood vessels; making the heart work harder and beat faster.

choreograph (KOR-ee-uh-graf)—Arranging the routines and steps of dances.

convenience (kun-VEEN-yens)—Anything that saves time or makes something easier.

endurance (en-DOO-rens)—The ability or strength to do something difficult for a long period of time.

guru (gur-oo)—A person who is very knowledgeable about a particular subject.

implement (IM-pluh-ment)—To fulfill, perform, or carry out something.

infomercial (IN-fo-mur-shel)—A long TV commercial that informs or instructs—often using celebrities—for the purpose of selling a product.

intensity (in-TEN-sa-tee)—Displaying great energy, strength, or concentration.,

leotard (LEE-uh-tahrd) —A skintight one-piece garment that covers the torso and often the arms, worn by dancers and gymnasts.

political activist (puh-LIT-i-kel AK-tuh-vist)—A person who works to bring about political or social change.

simulation (sim-yuh-LA-shun)—Imitating and looking or behaving like something else.

televangelist (tel-i-VAN-juh-list)—A preacher who regularly conducts religious services on television.

Index

About the Author

Sue Davis Potts is a freelance writer from Huntingdon, Tennessee. She holds degrees in both written communication and elementary education and has spent over fifteen years in early-childhood education. She has been published in *Clubhouse* and *Clubhouse, Jr.* magazines.